Infinity Ends Soon

by

Joseph Avski

Translated by Mark McGraw

El Paso | Huntsville TX

א

Infinity Ends Soon

Translated by Mark McGraw

The Spanish version of this book was first published by Emecé Colombia on January 1, 2015. ISBN: 978-9584243638

Mouthfeel Press is an indie press publishing works in English and Spanish by new and established poets. We publish poetry, fiction, and non-fiction. Our books are available through our website, Amazon.com, Bookshop.org, and other online and independent bookseller, or at author's readings.

Cover Design: Karen Dreher and Natalia Arreola
Cover Graphic: Roksolana Fursa via Canva.com

Contact information:

Mouthfeelbooks.com
Info.mouthfeelbooks@gmail.com

ISBN: 978-1-957840-01-7
Library of Congress Control Number: 20222945701

Published in the United States, 2023

First Printing in English
$16

א

Infinity Ends Soon

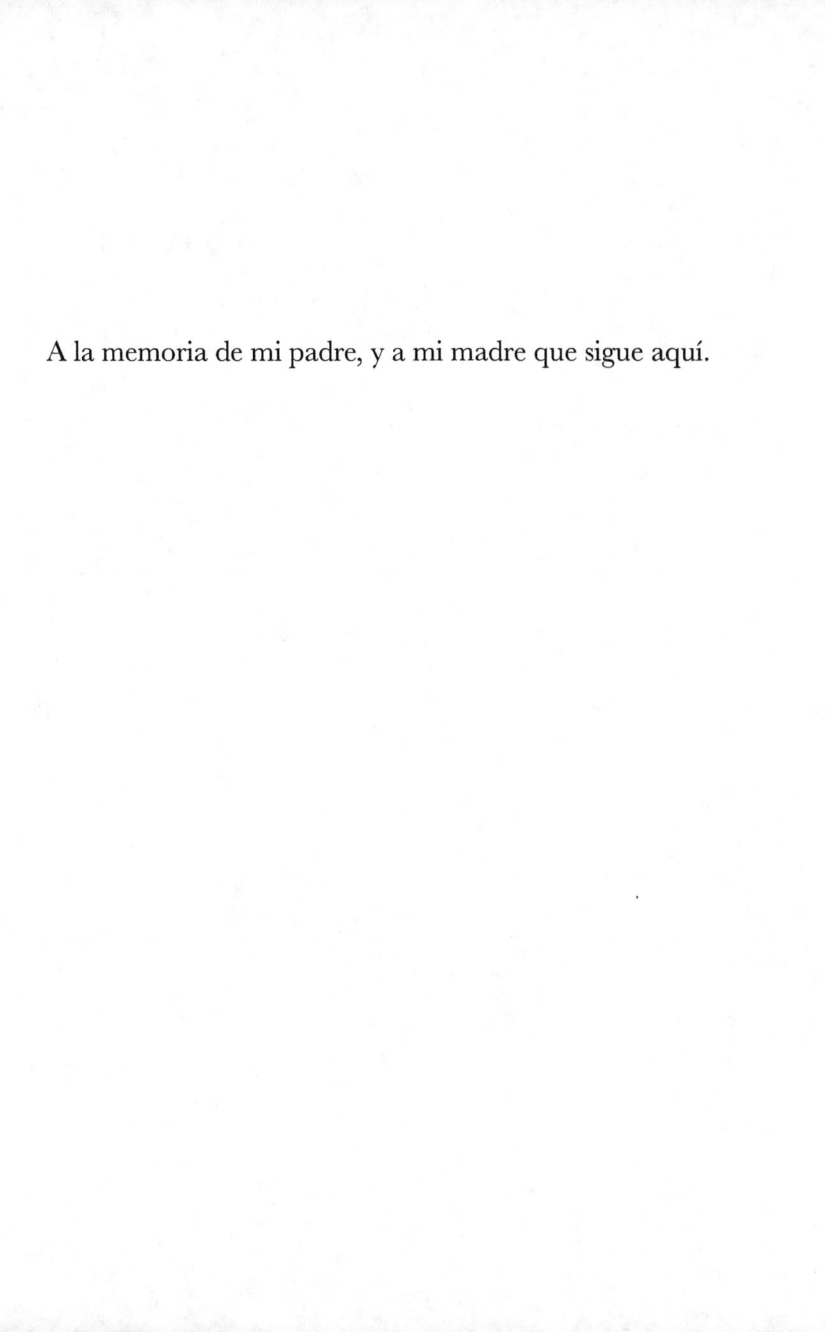

A la memoria de mi padre, y a mi madre que sigue aquí.

In that time the whole world spoke the same language. One day they said to each other, “Let’s make bricks and cure them in the fire.” So, they used bricks instead of stones and natural asphalt instead of mortar. After, they said, “Come; let us build a city and a tower that reaches to heaven.” But the Lord came down to see the city and the tower that the men were building, and thought, “They are a single people and speak one language, that is why they have started this work, and now they won’t stop for anything in the world. It is best that we come down and confuse their language, so that they do not understand each other.” And so it was that the Lord dispersed them through all the world, and they stopped building the city.”

Genesis 11:1-8

א

Man is equally incapable of seeing the
nothing from which he comes and the
infinity into which he is launched.

Blaise Pascal

As soon as I entered the hallway, I remembered a Gabriel García Márquez story in which a woman goes into an insane asylum to use the phone and they think she's an inmate and they don't let her leave. I imagined myself trapped here, going up and down this same hallway every day explaining that I was not crazy, or at least not so crazy that I needed to be locked up, and that I only wanted to continue researching the poet Raúl Gómez Jattin. That's how it is; sometimes memory is a shallow grave, sometimes the hallway of an insane asylum. Maybe because of the distraction, it took me a while to realize that the windows were closed despite the damn summer heat consuming Montería and that the heat fermented the air, giving it a smell of dirty clothes. Behind the window was an iron grid speckled with pigeon shit and soot. The security was exaggerated, I thought. These crazies couldn't be any more dangerous than a Colombian politician on the campaign trail. A nurse walked in front of me, indifferent to the heat, absorbed in the text messages on his cell phone. At the end of the hallway, he opened a door and waited for me to enter.

It was a clean and organized office, purified by the air conditioning and the antiseptic smell of an air freshener. The light poured in through the window and splashed across the desktop, but it wasn't able to sneak up on the realm of insanity. Something fatal resisted being illuminated.

I sat on one of the three seats in front of the desk and looked at the diplomas on the walls. Purely driven by my compulsion to read I got up again and approached the bookshelves with the optimism of an explorer. Most of the books were scientific texts on psychology and psychiatry, but there were also some books of literature, some of which were the ones that drove Don Quixote mad. This doctor could very well be as crazy as the Manchegan and believe he's a psychiatrist to right wrongs. A few minutes later, Dr. Urbino entered and greeted me with the quaint mannerisms of days gone by. Before I could take my seat again, a nurse with a bloodless face opened another door and Marcos entered.

"Avski? No, no, no!" shouted Marcos, surprised. "It can't be! Avski? Ha ha ha. What happened to you? Excuse me for saying it, but it looks like the age truck ran you over . . . ha ha ha . . . you look thirty-five."

I was thirty-four years old.

"Life," I said, as I approached him. "It never stops and shits on us all."

He wore a grimy robe over his clothing. It was strange to see him like that because Marcos is one of the most scrupulous dressers I've ever known in my life. He never went out without having his hair combed, his shoes shined, or putting on cologne. It would take him weeks to select a new hairstyle, all the while wearing out his friends with questions. The rest of us, the ones the whole town referred to as "metalheads," had long hair or green hair, cargo shorts and ripped jeans and the same flannel shirts that kept Kurt Cobain warm in Seattle but only cooked our guts more in the brutal Montería heat. Marcos, on the other hand, wore leather shoes and always had his shirt tucked in. He was the first person I ever knew who counted calories before his twentieth birthday. One day he confessed to me that he was incapable of making friends with a person who was too ugly or messy in appearance.

"Do you realize your friends are punks?" I had asked him.

"That's different."

Now he looked prematurely aged, tired like a soldier who returns from war. His skin had dark marks of poor health and he was missing a lower tooth, although it didn't seem to matter to him because he talked while showing his teeth without any self-consciousness.

Marcos, you're going to shit, I thought when I saw him.

The doctor brought us to a small patio with a couple of cement tables and a jasmine garden that no one watered, but the flowers refused to die despite the stupefying heat. The tables were under the shade of two trees: a mango and a hundred-year-old Bengal almond.

"I'll leave you alone," said the doctor as he excused himself with the dusty look of someone who dedicated his life to the useless fight against insanity. "But before I go, if it's all right, I'd like to have a word with Mr. Avski."

I returned with the doctor to the patio entrance. Next to the gate, he explained to me some behaviors that I would note in Marcos and how I should react. He also gave me his schedule in case I needed to speak to him later. I thanked him and went back to the table. Marcos had his back to me, distracted by an iguana climbing the mango tree and escaping the asylum over the edge of the back wall.

"That son of a bitch iguana got the green light. Do you think he's OK in the head?" I said, looking at the animal.

Marcos turned around, confused. He looked at me and grunted, stupefied, "Avski? No, no, no! It can't be! Ha ha ha."

The iguana nodded in the direction of the sun and went down the wall toward the outside world.

"What are you doing here? Excuse me for saying this, but it looks like they've put years in your soup . . . ha ha ha . . . you look like you're thirty."

"Well, shit, life always wants to keep giving us the green light," I answered without enthusiasm.

I tried not to look at the gap in his teeth. I wouldn't have recognized him even if we had run into each other on the street. His deterioration was much worse than a simple process of physical decline. He had an empty look, like an ancestral warrior tired from inhabiting the kingdoms of death.

I tried to ask him about his parents, but he interrupted me. He explained that he had made important advances in his research, and without giving me time to respond, he started on his first diatribe.

"There's a deep relation between the problems of self-reference and infinity. Think about two mirrors facing each other that create the image of an unending tunnel, made of chambers that don't exist, because each mirror reflects a reflection, the image of what never existed . . . see, Avski?"

"Marcos, I didn't come to talk about that."

"That's why people like Aristotle, Gauss, and Poincaré didn't believe in infinity." he continued.

"Maybe you're right," I answered. "In reality, everything in nature has an end, no matter how immeasurable it may seem."

"It's true. In nature, infinity only shows itself as an insinuation, a promise that can never be fulfilled. That's the tragedy behind Zeno's paradoxes: happiness, love, sexual pleasure, the tortoise that chases Achilles; they're always a step ahead, and no matter how many steps you take, you always need one more. But nature doesn't impose the limits of reality. Real infinity exists if it could be imagined, if it could be dreamed like Cantor dreamed it. The real home of infinity is in the heart of man," responded Marcos.

"Wow! Maybe your thing isn't mathematics, but intellectual poetry for housewives who read Paulo Coelho."

"You might think it´s funny, but it's true. Infinity, like poetry, doesn't exist in nature. Nevertheless, infinity is everywhere, in everything. Think about language, for example. If I say,

THE FOLLOWING PHRASE IS FALSE

And then I say,

THE PREVIOUS PHRASE IS TRUE.

Do you see? I can understand it as a contradiction or an infinite loop: two mirrors facing each other. It's everywhere, Avski, but people refuse to see it. They ignore it. That's what happened to Cantor. You know who Cantor is, right?"

He had told me about him thousands of times.

"Marcos, I didn't come to talk about . . ."

"Well, that's what happened to him. He saw infinity in full light while it scared everyone else. Understand that even God himself was afraid when they were building a tower in Babel to touch infinity. Look at the Greeks; all you have to do is read Zeno's paradoxes to realize how terrified they were of infinity. It blinded them, you understand? Only the great ones have seen infinity, like William Blake. Jealous people who couldn't comprehend the universe also hated him."

Before I could interrupt him, he started to recite:

"'See the World in a Grain of Sand

and Heaven in a Wild Flower

Hold Infinity in the palm of your hand

And Eternity in an hour.'

Beautiful, right? That's why they hated Blake, too, because he looked at infinity without fear. We're a race of cowards."

I remembered that Borges argued that all men are, in reality, one and that our destiny is singular. But, at least in that universe, the nut in the filthy white robe sitting in front of me was Georg Cantor, the great mathematician of infinity.

א

Leave it all again.
Take to the roads.
Roberto Bolaño

Sometimes memory is a shallow grave, sometimes it's a trip to the depths of night. I met Marcos in the early '90s in the damned hothouse of Montería. He lived with his grandmother and aunt in a house on 22nd street, opposite the Cuatro Caminos building. He never mentioned any other family members and never spoke of his parents, except to proudly say that his paternal grandfather was French.

In those days, we (the "metalheads:" the Orozco brothers, Jorge, Angel, Sebas, Luis, and, of course, Marcos), were convinced that we were the only intelligent people in the city. Montería was the ass of the world, and we were its only hope. We thought we were capable of anything. We had a punk band, made films with a video camera, and wrote poems about our insignificant miseries. Yet, all our projects were marked by one common characteristic: a miraculous mediocrity.

Marcos was one of the older ones.

He would brag about his great chess skills. He learned to play by reading a poorly translated Russian book that a National Public School professor had given him before he finished elementary school. He was probably the only adult who had taken an interest in him during his formative years. They would play two or three times a week after class. Before long, Marcos was at the same level as his professor. In reality, the professor was never a good player. Nevertheless, it gained Marcos some moderate fame as the child genius of his neighborhood and among the friends of his aunt and grandmother. Since then he tried to keep a playing partner, usually someone twenty or thirty years older who he would meet with once a week. He liked to play in silence under some bookish presumption that speaking took away from the game's elegance. The truth is that there was always a moment where formality bored him terribly, but the fool preferred to quietly put up with it.

Around 1993 he went to Medellín to study mathematics at the University of Antioquia. That transformed him into something of a local celebrity. At any given time, everyone, including people who barely knew him, would talk about him, admiring his intelligence, overtaken by the frivolity of pride in someone else's achievement.

During vacations Marcos returned to Montería and integrated himself into our routine. It was about that time that we formed the street art collective Memín 2099. We went out on Mondays or Tuesdays, when there was less vigilance, to cover the city's walls with graffiti. We would criticize the paramilitary culture quietly taking over society, the corruption of the local politicians, and the lack of commitment to education and culture. We were sure that our message was going to transform the city.

Naivety is a fault that is cured with time and beatings.

There soon appeared another graffiti group that called itself Onix, and a little war broke out between the two groups. All of our political discontent and cultural proposal were relegated to a secondary concern. Until then Marcos had not been very interested in Memín 2099. The crusades against injustice and the defense of education weren't the least bit interesting to him, but the rivalry with Onix was principally musical and it got his attention. They represented rap while we carried the torch for rock. In just a few days, Marcos took charge of the rivalry and covered the city with allusions to totalitarianism taken from Pink Floyd's *The Wall.*

No one agreed.

"Someone like Fujimori is what we need in this country," he said.

"A squatty guy?"

Soon after that we met Onix. They were three young out-of-towners who had arrived in Montería a year prior. We agreed to continue with the public antagonism, although we became good friends and even went out a few times to paint the city, even as Marcos held a grudge against them.

One night the three Onix guys showed up at the flat roof of the Garcés building, where we were to meet before going out to paint, and they warned us not to go out. Two nights before they had been arrested near the old Casa de Cultura, which had been transformed into a discotheque. From their cell they heard the police celebrating because they had captured "the Memín guerillas." The Onix boys told them they were mistaken, that they were our rivals and they proved it by showing a stencil of their signature.

The cops made them sign a declaration that said they weren't Memín 2099 and were told they would spend the night in jail anyway to cure them of their bad habits. The next morning, when they were let out, one of the policemen came up to them and warned them to stop painting graffiti, and that if the paramilitaries had found them that night instead of the police, they would have killed them without asking who they were. He said the bosses wanted the Memín boys disappeared.

That was the end of Memín 2099.

Those were the days when the gods of death got stronger in the city's fake peace, the days when we felt so strongly that we had to blow up the bedrock of society that we had bet our lives on art, literature, music, and science. It was an "all-in" bet in a poetic sense. We were destined to renew everything and return it to the very center of the life of man. We all had our obsessions, the pillars of our delirium. For Marcos, they were the mathematician Georg Cantor and *The Wall* by Pink Floyd.

א

Where there is a solitary rock
without any inscription,
where oblivion lives,
there will be my grave.
Gustavo Adolfo Bécquer

Marcos had been admitted to the San Pablo Hospital in Montería two years before. The diagnosis indicated three major illnesses: severe amnesia, a profound time perception disorder that kept him from being able to differentiate the past from the present, and a grave deterioration of his short-term memory.

Despite it all, life does indeed stop or at least creates the illusion that it is stopping. Sometimes memory is a shallow grave, sometimes it's a straitjacket. People get gummed up in the molasses of every day while time passes without warning. Ten years slip by without one realizing it. Family members die, friends move away, love takes a step back every day until it disappears, and life shits on us like a street pigeon on the facade of a building.

For Marcos, life had stopped a long ago, at the end of the '90s. Those were the days of Pastrana and the peace process with the FARC, the Armenia earthquake, and the unpunished assassination of Jaime Garzón. He had no consciousness of the fifteen years that had passed since then, no remembrance whatsoever, not a single trace in the trash can of his memories. Nevertheless, he showed all the relentless scars of the persistence of time. He lived in the unconsciousness of an eternal present, like those fish that eat so much they explode and die because they forget they are full.

Although life stalls, time doesn't stop. The years pass, and life and history pass. Maybe the only things the forgotten times had left him were physical marks and emotional scars, many of which he couldn't even recognize. He looked fifteen, maybe twenty years older than he was. Not only was he missing a tooth, but it also seemed like the rest were about to fall out. He walked hunched over, as if he carried an ancestral weight on his shoulders too large for a man in this age of digital trinkets. His voice sounded opaque, as if it traveled a long way through time from the happy years in which he didn't have to forget to live. An arduous symmetry united his empty head and the urgency with which his body aged, as if the physical decay paid the debt for his unserviceable memory.

"Marcos, what did your father do?" I asked him.

"My father read Borges, did you know?"

"I didn't know, but what did he do? What did he do for a living?"

"Did I ever tell you that his father, or that would be my grandfather, was French?"

"Yes, many times," I responded.

"Borges may be the only writer in Spanish who was interested in the problems of infinity."

"Is that why your father read him?"

"In reality, Borges didn't understand the nature of infinity. He, like the Greeks, understood infinity as something greater than the human capacity for enumeration, but it's much more."

"Was your father a literature professor or something?"

"People read 'The Aleph' and 'The Library of Babel' and think that Borges understood the concept of infinity, but the reality is no. What he describes in those stories are examples of the properties of the countless, not exactly of infinities," he explained.

"Marcos, why did your father read Borges?"

"The uncountable or the immeasurable is not the same as the infinite. In the first place …"

I remembered that Borges argues that no man lives in the past, and for certain, no one lives in the future. He concludes that we all live in the present, our ancestors and the generations to come. We're all contemporaries. Of course, Borges wasn't thinking about Marcos. This fool lives in the past and inhabits the future.

INFINITY ENDS SOON

The only time that is evasive for him is the present. He has no contemporaries; he is completely alone in a timeless garbage can. For Marcos the history of the world had stopped shortly before the turn of the century, and his life returned to zero every day since then. Nevertheless, the world continued, indifferent to the fool's forgetting.

א

They will see his face, and his name
will be on their foreheads.

Revelation 22:4

In 1856, at eleven years of age, Georg Cantor heard the Voice of God for the first time. His family was abandoning Saint Petersburg, later named Petrograd and then Leningrad, never to return. The Voice told him that his way should be mathematics, not music like he intended, the music that his mother shared, the music that made famous his maternal grandfather, the violinist Franz Böhm. In exchange, the Voice promised him that from that point on, He would guide him, He would light the darkness, and

He would comfort him in his loneliness.

The boy asked to see his guardian's face, but the Voice responded that His face could not yet be seen by man. He promised that he would see Him one day and that they would hate him for it. He would only reveal a glance, a small gesture of intolerable brilliance, an imperfect reflection that was an image of infinity. The boy believed that it was rotating and later understood that the movement was an illusion produced by the dizzying visions enclosed. It was just a spark of light, but the whole universe was contained in its brilliance. Everything was infinite things, seen from every point in the universe. He saw reflected the populous sea, the sunrise and the afternoon, the multitudes of America. He saw bunches of fruit, tobacco, steam, veins of metal, and every one of the infinite details of the morning light's fragmented lace as it passed through snowbanks. He saw convex equatorial deserts and each grain of sand. He saw Zeno next to an immobile arrow and Achilles running lazily behind a turtle. He saw his grandfather's violinist hands rotting below the ground, far from his instrument.

He saw the ruins of a tower in Babel, the cycles of reincarnation, and the circles of time. He saw that every man is contained in each of his cells and he couldn´t explain it to himself. He simultaneously saw every one of the infinite numbers that men called Naturals; he saw much more complex numbers that exceeded in their counting the sum of the events, the objects, and the forms of the universe itself. He saw the unmeasurable emptiness of the atom and interstellar space, night and day, the midsummer heat and the perpetual ice, and in Alkmaar's cabinet, he saw a terrestrial globe between two mirrors that multiplied without end. He saw the burning heart of the sun and the distant sun billions of times larger and hotter. He saw a man in Argentina fascinated with mirrors and labyrinths who, many years later, would allege to have seen the same thing his eyes were seeing. He saw that man weep because his eyes had seen the secret and conjectural object, whose name men usurped but no man had looked at: the face of infinity.

The vision left the boy exhausted and he slept.

Georg grew, studied, and married.

Everything turned out familiar to him for the rest of his life, even though he had almost completely forgot the fantastic vision, to the point that he believed it to be a martingale of his juvenile imagination. Sometimes memory is a shallow grave, sometimes a black abyss where all the forms of the universe are hidden.

א

The darker the night, the brighter
the stars, the deeper the grief,
the closer God is!

Fyodor Dostoyevsky

What hath night to do with sleep?
John Milton

The years pass, life and death passes, and the dreadful history of a country falls off a ledge. One hand writes the other punches. In March of 1997, I went to live in Medellín and entered the University of Antioquia to study physics. In those days, San José de Apartadó was declared a "Community of Peace" and the FARC responded by decapitating four people near there and, months later, killing five Koreguaje natives in Caquetá Department. Also, the paramilitaries under Carlos Castaño and Salvatore Mancuso massacred fourteen people in El Carmen de Viboral, and a still undetermined number of people in the Mapiripán massacre. It was also around the time that Diomedes Díaz threw the cadaver of Doris Adriana Niño in the trash.

I came to live in the Fatima neighborhood at the house of an aunt who looked suspiciously at my urgency to experience everything the new city offered me. It was a big house full of religious paintings that looked at me with resentment every time I entered. Fatima was, in those days, a neighborhood of sanctimonious old women and corner drunks who bent their elbows in the name of the Holy Catholic Church and the Conservative Party. A few blocks from my aunt´s house was the Church of Our Lady of Fatima, where she spent most of her time.

Marcos lived close to there. He shared a house with other students next to the First Park of Laureles, so it was common for one of us to walk to the other´s house. Back then I doubted that Marcos could graduate as a mathematician. He had failed some classes and had to withdraw from others due to poor performance. After three and a half years in Medellín, he had still not finished his second-year classes.

That year we spent more time together than any other. We explored the downtown bars with the meticulousness of pilgrims. We always carried cheap coke in our pockets and had an unbreakable agreement to hold out using until they had kicked us out of all the places. Some nights we´d start at the Homero Manzi, a tango bar frequented by old guys trapped in the haze of the '50s. We made friends with a group of retired lawyers. They all had slicked-back hair and wore black coats and ties, with white handkerchiefs delicately showing above the left breast pocket. They bought our drink and, in exchange, we listened to their dusty stories. We pretended to find in their diatribes a profound, long-lost relevance that probably never existed. After a few free drinks, we´d go to the bathroom to powder our noses and continue on with our pilgrimage.

We´d leave the Homero Manzi and go down by Pichinha to the Bomboná Towers bars. The Art Institute students were always there, more fans of tequila than rum or moonshine. After a few drinks with the artists, we´d go up by Girardot or Palo Street until La Playa Avenue. On the way, we'd stop for an emergency drink in one of the neon-lit cantinas. On La Playa Avenue, the music and taste in liquor improved greatly. We´d start with the pertinent libations in the cellars on the right side of the sidewalk until we got to the Fine Arts Palace. From there, we'd go down again toward El Guanábano. The route was basically a trip through the rhythms of the Antilles and through the tastes of its nectars. The night would continue in El Eslabón Prendido, where the salsa musicians were always ready to share a rum and a joint. At that point, we´d leave Antillean music and head for rock. We´d go down by Maracaibo Street, passing the Colombo Americano Center, until we got to Cancielo. The crowd there preferred beer over strong liquors, with marijuana and coke. But by two in the morning, the darkest hour, they would have thrown us out of all the places and then we´d need to devise a plan to squander what was left of the night.

Some nights we´d end up in Periodista Park, skimming coins for a drink or a late-hour joint. We´d wake up there surrounded by bums, knife fighters, small-time pushers, drunks, and criminals. Marcos would be transformed in that environment. His hostile attitude was modified in the way he got along with foreigners. He knew most of the drug dealers and knife fighters around the park. He enjoyed talking with them, engaging them under the slightest pretext. But he didn't stop being pedantic even if he was friendlier and much more courteous than usual. He´d use the most obscure language, more sibylline than usual. He enjoyed it when they´d interrupt him to ask what this or that word meant. I was always afraid that his extreme pedantry would bring on problems, but it never happened. Marcos shined next to the street folks.

I preferred to wake up in the apartment of Maria Isabel, the wandering night owl. Her hideout was on the top floor of a tower off Girardot Avenue, just a few streets from Periodista Park. Her apartment gave off the same decadent refinement as the rest of the building. She liked to wake up surrounded by drunk college students who stole her books and screwed in the bathroom. At one time or another, each of us wound up in her bedroom and we loved her, and we´d laugh out loud thanks to her potent sex still smoking despite her fifty well-lived years. We all had stormy nights and sandy mornings there. We all had lovers and friends among the visitors who frequented Maria Isabel´s apartment. All except Marcos. Women rejected the fool with more and more fervor, and friendship eluded him.

א

The closer to infinity,
the deeper in the guts of terror.
Gustave Flaubert

The years pass, and life and history pass. At the University of Berlin Georg studies with Leopold Kronecker, Karl Weierstrass, and Ernst Kummer. He is interested in number theory and writes his thesis on it. Shortly after his graduation, he is offered a position at the University of Halle, where he spends the rest of his life. He marries, has children, and sees death from a tower window.

I have had disturbing dreams, he writes in his diary. In them a shadow is transformed into the night, some men change their faces, others wear masks with macabre grimaces, some laugh, and others go crazy. One number is transformed into many, one point into a line, and one gesture into a life.

I am unable to identify the meaning of these visions, if they have any.

Georg continued alert, especially on cold nights when the silence is deeper, but the Voice only revealed small details. He had waited for seventeen years, since the days when he was a child leaving Russia. Mathematics come effortlessly to him, without the work required of others but without ingeniousness. He continues his work on number theory, and waits. He is always close to the steps the Voice recommends to him, always close to a formless form, to a name without a name, to a number the numbers can´t name. Later he dedicates himself to trigonometric series, the same ones that fascinated Jacques Bernoulli in the 17th century because they express a simple number as an infinite sum. So there the immense is hidden in the small, the innumerable in the outline of a smile.

INFINITY ENDS SOON

In 1873 Georg´s faith fades. The Voice is manifested everywhere, but there is not a single word for him. Instead, the Voice whispers to Tchaikovsky the melody of *The Storm*. He orders the American army to massacre Indians in His name; He turns into opium and fog in the streets of London to dictate "A Season in Hell" to Arthur Rimbaud, and He reveals to James Clerk Maxwell the arcane language of the first words of creation.

Georg waits.

He listens.

One of the primary problems in talking about infinite collections is comparing them. Georg wondered how to know that the sets (1,2,3) and (A,B,C) have the same number of elements. The answer is simple: if there is a one-to-one relation, without any leftover or missing elements in any sets.

We connect 1 with A,

2 with B,

3 with C.

The way to compare infinite sets should be the same. Then Georg took a section, the Odd numbers (1,3,5,7,9 . . .) and compared them with the Naturals (1,2,3,4,5 . . .). He wondered if one set would be larger than the other. The obvious answer that crosses the minds of those of us accustomed to looking at the floor is that there are half as many Odd numbers as Naturals. Between 1 and 10, there are 5 Odds and 10 Naturals. Between 1 and a million, there are a half million Odds and a million Naturals. The labyrinths of logic indicate that the difference would continue the same to infinity, that Natural numbers would always be twice the Odds, but Georg doesn't feel satisfied with this answer. After all, both sets are infinite, both are the size of God, and he has seen the eye that contains the stars and the grains of sand, the atoms and all their parts, the writing and the music, the time and it´s secret mechanism.

If he was capable of putting the two sets in relation whereby each natural number corresponded to one and only one of the Odd numbers, without any number in either set being left out, then he would have demonstrated that both sets have the same quantity of elements.

1 corresponds to 1,

2 to 3,

3 to 5,

4 to 7,

5 to 9,

6 to 11,

and so forth, successively to infinity.

He remembered Aristotle and understood that he was wrong: all is not greater than the sum of its parts. Not always. Sometimes the parts are as atrocious as the total. Maybe there exists a drop of water as deep as the ocean, an atom that extends all the way to the very borders of the universe.

א

How few days go to make up a century.

Bram Stoker

Another year passes, life, confusion, the terrible history of Colombia and the discrete imperfection of mathematics pass. In those days, Marcos started to move away from our night routine and entered a vortex of failed relationships to which he surrendered himself with a debauchery that was unusual for him. He came out of all of them thrashed. If it were not for how real his pain seemed, I would have thought that his misadventures in love were a lie.

I never personally met any of these women, and I only

remember concrete details about two, although he must have had five or six romances during that time. They all had the same outstanding traits. They were actresses, poets, philosophers, and mathematicians, played violin and did modern dance, recited Rimbaud in French, or had been jugglers in Cirque du Soleil.

Every time Marcos started or ended a new relationship, he´d come to my house and would ask me to walk with him for a little bit. The route always included the area around Our Lady of Fatima Church. It gave him pleasure to pass next to the temple and make fun of the faithful. He´d use this theatrical voice and talk louder than necessary, so the passersby could hear him. The farce bothered me, mainly because his arguments were commonplace for a Good Friday atheist. Of course, I was much more tolerant at that time than I am now. I still had not yet suffered the majestic collection of foolishness repeated by the creationists nor the chilling excesses of religious folk smothered in politics. After his theological discourse, Marcos would pivot to subjects of love, communication, and sexuality. If it had to do with a breakup or the beginning of a relationship, I had to withstand a detailed list of dreams and expectations, or a compendium of bitterness and disappointment.

One afternoon Marcos arrived at my aunt´s house, especially somber. By then, I was already a little tired of his pathos, but he seemed so sad I decided to accompany him one more time. We went out toward the church, but unlike on other occasions, Marcos stayed quiet. We walked in silence for a long while. I felt happy not to have to put up with his dramatic droning. After a few blocks, I even forgot that we were together. Shortly before getting back to the house, while we were passing next to the church again, Marcos broke the silence:

"Do you know what I´d want to recover from my childhood if I could?"

"Ah? What?" I was so distracted that I didn´t understand him the first time.

"Do you know what I´d want to recover from my childhood if

I could?" he repeated.

"What?"

"Faith in God."

א

Mathematics, rightly viewed,
possesses not only truth, but supreme beauty -
a beauty cold and austere like that of a sculpture....
Bertrand Russell

Open the door through which we
can see the infinite firmament....
Giordano Bruno

Days pass, life and history pass. Georg carries out his responsibilities as a professor at the University of Halle but secretly feels that his talent merits a more prestigious institution. He trusted that once the Voice spoke to him clearly and revealed its secrets, the fundamentals of mathematics would be so shaken that only the ruins of Aldebaran would be left of the ancient temples. Then the best universities in Germany would seek him out. Maybe Berlin or Göttingen would be in his future.

In those years, he read the ridiculous Thomas Aquinas, who believed that continuity was made neither by an infinite number of parts nor by a finite number. Georg saw in that answer the same fear as his contemporaries. They all preferred a foolish affirmation instead of seeing the innumerable eyes of God watching men from the vastness of a limitless ocean of time.

He also reads Aristotle and Epicurus, who have opposite opinions about continuity. There he looks for the bricks for his new Tower of Babel. Epicurus imagined continuity as made up of finite and indivisible parts called atom, but Georg felt the transit to continuity from atoms proposes a contradictory logic. Aristotle believes that there are two types of infinity: a real and unattainable infinity, a product of the imagination, inexistent in nature, impossible to know, unthinkable, unnamable like the jaws of the Evil One; and another potential infinity, made of finite parts that belong to a borderless set where there is always a new part to explore, like the possibility of a route no one travels. Ever since Aristotle's real infinity was declared prohibited territory, it's as if its study opened the doors of hell.

Georg waits.

He listens.

In those days he was interested in the problem of continuity. How is it possible, he wondered, that a line without gaps is made of numeric points? The difficulty was rooted in this: any pair of points we choose always allows a space between them. It doesn't matter how close they may be, they never get sufficiently close to each other. If we don't know the neighbor of any number, how do we know that it even exists?

Maybe continuity is an illusion.

It's possible, writes Georg that the problem is born out of the way we understand numbers. Maybe the Integers, the Rationals, and the Irrationals conjecture very distinct natures, and even different sizes in their infinity. Recently I've caught myself thinking about the Integers like stones in a jar. Then I imagine the Rationals like sand filling the empty spaces between the stones, but leaving tiny spaces between one grain and another. Lastly, I contemplate the Irrationals like water poured over the sand, filling each space left in the previously placed material.

Georg decides to rummage through the nature of Rational numbers, which can be written like a quotient of two Integers, or as a finite or periodical decimal number. They seem infinitely more abundant than the Naturals, dense to the point of fatigue, untamable and somber. Just between 1 and 2 there is an infinity. Also, between 1.1 and 1.2, infinite Rationals pile up like snakes in a nest. It doesn't matter how close they are, whether they be 1.0000001 and 1.0000002 or 1.0000000000000000001 and 1.0000000000000000002, there is always space to accommodate many more infinities. To understand them better Georg, decides to compare them with Naturals. For that, he needs to find a method that puts them in some kind of relation, like he had done with the

Odds. It is easy to start:

1 corresponds to 1, but it is impossible to choose the second element; whichever one you may choose, let's say 1.1, infinite Rationals are forgotten in between. For the Odds, it is clear that after 1 follows 3, for the Primes it is clear that 2 is followed by 3, and 3 is followed by 5, but there is no way to find the neighbor of 1.0 or 2/3, no matter how close they may be. Georg conjectures that the problem of order cannot be resolved, so he must orient his energy on finding a form to include all the Rational numbers independent of order and vicinity. It is enough to achieve a list that contains them all.

At night he is assaulted by disturbing dreams. In all of them a face is conjured with the features of all men past and future, with untold miseries under his eyelids and joy that drips from his smile. However, he knows that that multiform man is no more than his own image bent over a desk working on his craft. He dreams about the delicate persistence of the Hebrew numerologists and the dark secrets of the Cabala. He observes his grandfather's hand buried in the ground, far from his violin, and next to the hand the secret scripture of the cabalists who also found God in music and numbers. He sees multitudes arguing in the original language of Babel used by the men who decided to build a tower to reach heaven. A voice is raised above them all, the Voice of the infinite face, and it orders him to immediately return to work.

Upon returning to his vigil Georg builds a catalogue that contains all the Rational numbers just as he saw them populate the levels of the impious tower.

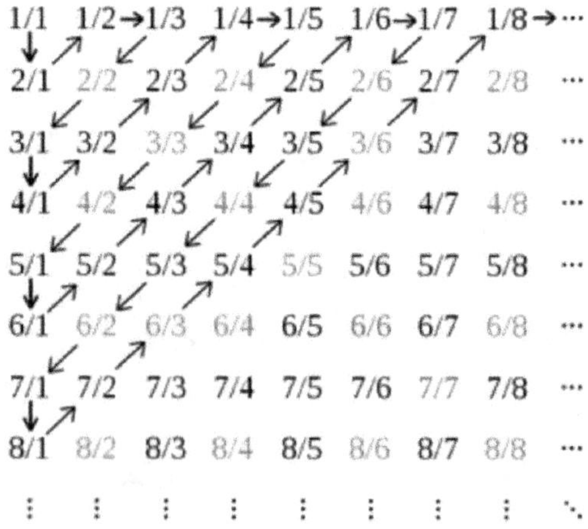

In the table no Rational is missing; each and every one is there. The repeated numbers are written in bold, ensuring that 2/2 and 3/3 and 4/4 are all one, and 1/2 and 2/4 and 3/6 are all a half. All that was left was to create a correspondence that related each number of the table, avoiding repetitions, with a Natural number. Following the arrows he started:

To 1 corresponds 1,

to 2 corresponds 2,

to 3 corresponds 1/2,

to 4 corresponds 1/3,

to 5 corresponds 3 because 2/2 is one, a reiteration of one,

to 6 corresponds 4,

to 7 corresponds 3/2,

. . .

No Rational number is left out, no matter how small or perverse it may be.

Georg concludes that there are as many Rationals as Naturals, that the Rationals' suffocating density is nothing more than an illusion produced by our tiny experience; and our intuition is insufficient when trying to understand God. The procedure is elegant and devastating, defiant to traditional mathematics. Many are threatened by the conclusion. They believe that logic is broken to pieces before their eyes and that it is their duty to defend the pillars of reason. They must reject the fabrications of this Cantor, because if they don't, the belief in intuition will be destroyed forever. Sometimes memory is a deep grave, sometimes it is a room where chains are broken.

Whoever fights monsters should see to it
that in the process he does not become a monster.
And if you gaze long enough into an abyss,
the abyss will gaze back at you.
Friedrich Nietzsche

The longest and tortuous of his relations at that time was with Margot Jiménez. Like all the previous ones, Margot was an archetype of intellectual virtues. She studied philosophy and literature at the Pontifical Bolivarian University and was a theater actress. He had met her after a production of *Romeo and Juliet* that had been adapted to show the violence between rival gangs in the poor neighborhoods of Medellín. Margot was the lead actress, the spoiled Capulet's daughter. Marcos congratulated her after the production and asked her to have coffee with him in El Acontista.

"You're probably falling in love with the insufferable Juliet and not with Margot. She's your type," I told him.

"Of course not," he responded. "That thing of falling in love with literary characters only happens to you writers."

During his relationship with Margot, Marcos would disappear for long periods and would reappear in an unbearably bad mood. When he returned, he would show a hateful emotional dependence that he had never shown before. He would ask me to listen to him; he confessed that he needed someone to talk to, showing me his most vulnerable side. Then my affection for Marcos was not like during the sunny days of Montería, when it was enough to know that he was another weirdo living in an intolerant society to make him feel like a brother to me. Now, to hear him and know his most human side was precisely the last thing I wanted.

One night he confessed that he felt pleasure for the first time with Margot. Real pleasure, he clarified.

"Perfect sexuality isn't between man and woman, but between human beings who love each other," he added.

"Ricardo Arjona couldn't have said it any worse," I told him. "That woman has turned you into a total poet."

He called her Petit Margot and told me the name had to do with an intellectual joke that I never understood. He told me about their plans to travel around Guajira, write a book together, take weekly photos for twenty years, and move to Australia.

"In Sidney there's a group of impressive mathematicians working in my area. I'm sure that in a few years it will be one of the most important research centers on infinity. Just imagine all I could develop in an environment like that, while here the mediocrity around has me stagnated."

"No doubt. And just imagine everything those mathematicians can do over there if you don't bother them."

"Ha ha, Avski. It's also a great opportunity for my Petit.

Australia is about to turn into the mecca of film. Look at what is going on with Nicole Kidman and Baz Luhrmann. There will be a lot of opportunities over there to develop her acting career."

One night Marcos called me and asked me to meet him in a bar. I came up with excuses. I told him I was tired, didn't have time and had to study. It was all to no end. He didn't give up until I accepted. As a last resort I told him I didn't even have money for the bus, so he offered to pay for a round trip taxi. His answer alarmed me since I never knew anyone as stingy with money as Marcos.

When I got to the bar, he didn't even say hello.

"She humiliated me, on purpose . . . she humiliated me. The Petite Margot, the Petite little whore," he said.

He didn't want to explain what had happened. Although in those days, he always wanted to talk about personal issues, until then he had been particularly reserved about the details of his relationship with Margot. He mentioned disconnected episodes:

parts of a conversation, gestures, and insults. After a while he stood up and gave me a few bills, "It's late. This will be enough to pay the bill and your taxi home."

After that incident he disappeared again. I supposed that everything had been fixed and that he would leave me peacefully.

No way, José.

Things between them had been resolved, but after a fling of a few days, Marcos had decided to not stay away like in previous times. A couple of weeks later, he started calling me more urgently. He often tried to set up meetings, to which I always responded with excuses. When we finally agreed on a date, he'd have a beer or a coffee and take off. He would often ask me about the old friends from our bohemian days and wound up advising me to grow up and get out of the world of nighttime excess.

Twice we got together so I could meet Petit Margot, and she didn't show up on both occasions. The first time Marcos explained that she was working on Pessoa's *O Marinheiro* at the Matacandelas

Theater, and that all rehearsals had her schedule out of whack.

"You can't imagine the talent and dedication of that woman," he told me. "That's the foundation of success, Avski, discipline, constancy. We can't keep believing in genius and inspiration. How many hours do you spend writing? How many on physics every day? If you really love what you do, you must give yourself to it, body and soul. She lives for the theater; it's what she dedicates all her time and energy to. I'd really like you to meet her because you could learn a lot from her. You're not going to make science progress by rolling from bar to bar."

"Don't worry, Marcos," I responded. "I have faith in the progress of science without my help."

The second time Marcos didn't justify her absence; he just started entertaining me with one of his stories about infinity. He told me about Nicholas of Cusa, a German priest educated in fifteenth-century Italy, who defended the idea that the universe was infinite. He argued that any person on earth sees the horizon at the same distance no matter where they are, so that any point can be seen as the center. In the same way, the earth seems to be in the center of the universe, not because it really is, but because being the infinite universe, any place seems to be the center. The poor fool became a cardinal, but his stubbornness about infinity, at a time when the Church didn't want to know anything about the subject, caused Pope Pius II to excommunicate him and he was imprisoned in 1460.

"Marcos, you didn't ask me to meet you here so you could tell me about some fucking lunatic. I have things to do. Is your woman coming or not?"

"I don't think so."

"Why?"

"That's just how she is."

He never talked about Australia again.

א

> Your servant is here among the people
> you have chosen, a great people,
> too numerous to count or number.
> I Kings 3:8

The Voice not only showed Georg that there were infinities as atrocious in the part as in the whole, that a drop of water contains the ocean, that a second compresses the history of all mankind, their miseries and their hopes, their fear of the infinite and time, it also showed him that some infinities are better than others, some larger, some smaller, some more just, others more drunk with the hatred of creation.

On November 29, 1873, Georg clearly hears the Voice of God.

Write.

This morning I heard His voice with unusual clarity. I wondered, Is God infinite in the same way as the Natural numbers? This question has distracted me all morning, and I have reached a satisfactory conclusion. Real infinity can only be talked about in three ways. The first is to refer to Him and his attributes: The Absolute Infinity. His mercy is infinite, His wisdom is infinite, and His love is infinite: *aeterno omnipotenti sive natura naturanta*. Second, in the way that it occurs in created nature, *concreto seu in natura naturata*. And third, in the way that it can be invoked in the abstract, formulated and understood by human intelligence.

The criticisms I have received, continued Georg, don't just accuse me of taking mathematics and science down the road of lies and errors, but rather of using my talents to blaspheme against the Creator. They are Catholics faithful to Rome, those who my mother and her family hold close to their hearts, otherwise pious men, who have so fervently led the campaign to discredit me. They accuse me of creating false idols since only God is infinite.

Nevertheless, the criticisms that surprise me the most are those of my colleagues. They appeal to Carl Friedrich Gauss and his prohibition of completed infinity in the realm of mathematics. Could it be that their use of infinity as a mental image be different from my abstract infinity? One is as real and meaningful as the other. Both allow us to understand and marvel at creation. By what mechanism did Gauss, a pious man who looked so far and so deeply into creation in a way that can only be seen with the help of Him, become so short-sighted as to ignore that the first form of infinity created us, gave us life and takes care of us; the second surrounds us in the form of time and space; and the third form inhabits the mind and spirit of man to remind us that our origin and our destiny is Him, the Absolute?

Is God infinite in the same way as the Naturals are, wonders Georg. Maybe a one-to-one correspondence between Natural and Real numbers doesn't exist, that is to say, one of the sets is larger than the other, more inhuman. Maybe there is something intimate in the continuous sets, in that closeness that leaves no space between the elements, that is unknown in the discrete numbers. Something deep and dark that not even infinity can level. Maybe not even death is the equalizer of men, maybe only astonishment and pain put them on the same level.

Again, his method was simple and devastating. He made a list of all the Real numbers between 0 and 1. No matter the order, no matter how the second element was selected after the first, all that mattered was that all the numbers between 0 and 1 were included. The list is something like this:

0.0233837392…

0.6383747931…

0.3576328938…

0.1462647383…

0.8256952417…

…

and so forth until all the Real numbers are listed.

Using the catalogue Georg decided to build a number that will be different from the first in the first digit (0), different from the second in the second digit (3), different from the third in the third digit (7), and so forth successively.

The first digit of the new number can be I, different from 0.

The second 4, different from 3.

The third 8, different from 7.

And so forth, until exhausting the list.

0.14830

This number that Georg imagined always differed from any number on the list by a digit and is nonetheless a real number between 0 and 1. The conclusion is that there cannot be a list of the Real numbers, no matter what method may be used to generate it because there will always be some elements left over.

In other words, the Real numbers are uncountable and the uncountable cannot be counted, just as the innumerable cannot be numbered. The Real numbers have another sized infinity, unmeasurable and incomparable with that of the Naturals, much rougher, more absurd, more majestic; they are a larger god, more powerful, more merciless when facing the infidels.

That same year the world economy collapsed as if scared by the incredible results Georg found. The Prolonged Depression, as it was called, goes on for almost six years until the summer of 1879. It is the first of three great world depressions during which the bankers enriched themselves and everyone else has been impoverished. During the six years of economic recession the Voice disappeared, as if the economy had something to do with metaphysical voices and the wickedness of infinity.

There are more things in Heaven and Earth,
Horatio, than are dreamt of in your philosophy.
William Shakespeare

One of the first signs of the beginning
of understanding is the wish to die.
Franz Kafka

Marcos was more active than ever in the University. He wanted to take several directed studies and pass them with an exam.

"Really, my problem with the University is the speed," he told me. "I learn much quicker than the others, but the classes are so slow I wind up getting distracted and I lose interest."

"No one would have imagined that that was the problem."

"Yeah, it's not so apparent, but now I know I can pass two or three times the number of classes per semester."

"Last semester you only passed one class, so if you manage to pass three times the classes, you'll still be two classes behind your slowest classmates."

He clarified that his purpose was to graduate in two or three years and move to Romania.

"Romania?"

Nicoleta was Romanian, white, Marcos emphasized, not gypsy. They had been seeing each other for five or six weeks, during which Romania was the center of Western Civilization for Marcos.

"She lived there with her grandparents a few years before returning to Colombia with her parents, and she told me it was the perfect place to live. When she lived there, she worked for Cirque du Soleil."

"If I didn't know you well," I said ironically. "I would think that all those women really existed."

"Avski, Avski, the world is not as small as you suppose," he responded, bewildered.

One night I had to put up with a recounting of the history of Dacia beginning with the fall of the Roman Empire, accompanied by traditional music from the Bacău province, where Nicoleta's grandparents were from. Marcos interrupted his story to give me a summary of the plot of every song and explained how much more beautiful Romanian was than Spanish. He offered to make me a copy and recommended that I listen to it in the mornings to start the day.

"That way you can learn a little Romanian for when you meet Nicoleta," he said.

He started to explain to me the Slavic influences on the complicated Romanian grammar, so I cut him off with the only argument I had handy: "Make me a copy." At that point, I really couldn't have given a fuck about the rich Romanian culture. At the end of his boring spiel he made me promise that I would think about moving to Bucharest after finishing my Physics degree, since the city was destined to turn into one of the most important scientific centers in the world.

"You read that in the horoscope."

"Avski, there's going to be a new Renaissance in Romania, believe me. Do you know what 'Romanian' means? It means in the Roman way. They were there at the heart of Western history from the beginning. When King Mihai I returns, the country will return to its roots. He is the cousin of the Queen of Denmark, the King of Norway, King Juan Carlos of Spain, the king of Sweden, and Queen Elizabeth II of England, understand? Those are the people who will be by his side. Romania will forget about that communist crap and about gypsies and Slavs and Muslims and will go back to being true Europe."

"What's so bad about gypsies and Muslims?"

"Muslims are invading Europe. They're disrespectful. They show up and don't make any effort to assimilate, as if everything were for them. Quite the opposite, they ask that laws be changed and that they get benefits and are guaranteed privileges, and if that doesn't happen, then they claim they're being discriminated against. They should go back to their countries; the civilized world doesn't need them."

"Too bad you weren't in charge when the Europeans came to America."

"It's not the same."

"I don't believe the Romanians are going to think it's the same. Especially when they see your brown face."

One night Marcos called me to go out for some beers. He was in a bad mood and barely talked. I was a little thrown off by his silence, or maybe just a little bored, and I asked him about Nicoleta. With a grim look on his face, he stared at me and said, "Avski, Avski, people don't always live happily ever after like they do in fairy tales."

"I thought they do in Romania," I responded.

After that I started to deliberately ignore him and did not call him back. I'd lie to him that I was busy. When we would meet, he'd talk about grandiloquent subjects. Suicide and freedom were his newest themes. As for me, his pretentious arguments shocked me and his superficial intellectual conversation wore me out. I didn't believe anything he told me, and I wasn't interested in his damned parish poet fantasies or his great mathematician delirium. One night he took out his billfold and showed me a razor blade.

"I carry it to remind myself that staying alive is my own decision," he told me.

"Use it," I told him. "Or it will rust on you."

א

Who can count the sands of the seas,
the raindrops and the days of eternity?
Sirach 1:2

In all things it is better to hope than to despair.
Johann Wolfgang von Goethe

At thirty-four Georg is named full professor at the University of Halle, an honor very few have received at such a young age. Nevertheless, Georg feels that much greater honors await him and that the most important mathematics departments in Germany will soon open their doors to him. Between 1879 and 1884, he hears the Voice more clearly than ever before or after in his life. It reveals to him what it had promised: its face—the very structure of the universe that no one had ever seen face to face. During those five years, Georg writes the gospel of infinity with a prophetic hand.

For a time, Georg believes there is a limit, a larger infinity than the others, an end to the useless vastness of numbers. That limit would be God who looks from eternity and, every now and then, sends his Voice to speak to abject sinners like him. That finding would have to silence his critics' voices, who would understand that no one like him had approached Him.

In his dreams the shadows transformed into nights, and at night children were transmuted into beasts, water into blood, and the history of reason into the monstrous chronicle of Europe's devastation. Some men change their faces, put on macabre masks, dance around the fire and worship golden oxen engraved with arcane symbols. Others walk among bodies or hide themselves in filthy trenches and laugh, seized by fever and dementia. Numbers multiply like the sins of men, geometric structures take the shape of the Devil's tricks, and the number of the Evil One is marked with fire on the foreheads of free men.

During the vigil Georg forgets the sinister meanings of his dreams and sits beneath the teardrop lamp in his study looking for the limit. For months he doesn't go out until he arrives at the terrible conclusion that an ultimate infinity from where God watches us does not exist. It doesn't matter how immense an infinity may be, there is always another even more ridiculous that expands without end, one even larger than the last, all immeasurable, foolishly incomprehensible to human understanding. No matter how ridiculous or absurd, it is always possible to find another larger infinity, a more majestic god. Georg found all the hierarchy of infinities infinite in itself. The Natural numbers we use to count, that surprise us so much, that are more than all the content in the universe, more than the days and the hours and the things and the atoms and the possible combinations, are barely the smallest of the infinities, the most insignificant.

Immediately, he writes to Julius Wilhelm Richard Dedekind, telling him his discovery, the blasphemy hidden in the artifices of mathematics. Hours later he decides not to send the letter, not to publish the forged finding until he can be much more certain. Confused, he goes out to walk along the Saale River. On the way it occurs to him to hide his findings like the Pythagoreans did. He would not be the one to set fire to his own cathedral. Sometimes memory is a shallow grave, sometimes it´s a dank, shady path next to a river.

From deep in the forest he hears the Voice that repeats the same question, "Is God infinite in the same way as the Natural numbers?"

Georg understands the true significance of his discovery.

When he returns to his study, he writes, I see it, but I don't believe it, to his friend Dedekind, who he had met the year before. He continues, this finding fills me with joy because it confirms my suspicions about two types of irreconcilable infinities that have confused Kant and Spinoza's disciples, otherwise just and brilliant men (as well as the new scholastic theologians who have accused me of defending the lies of pantheism to the point of weariness). The criticisms against me founded on this inaccuracy have not only created pain and moved us away from the only just end, which is to approach God through knowledge of his creation. I hope that with this new finding, the difference can be established beyond any misinterpretation. One is the Absolute, the infinity that describes God and His attributes, which is outside any mathematic formulation. The kindness of God cannot be rationally or spiritually determined. His grace and His mercy are so complete, so perfect, that they resist any measurement. What can be greater than the love of God? What can we compare it to without impoverishing it? The other is the infinity that merely goes beyond the finite, which I call transfinite, which is no more than a mathematic expression. My proof showing that this kind of infinity can always be enlarged makes confusion impossible. Any limit opposes the idea of God. There is no border beyond which is a prohibited region for Him, a place where grace, justice, and compassion disappear. Nothing escapes God, neither kindness nor evil, neither pain nor despair. God contains Himself, and all that is not Him. He cannot be good without being evil. He cannot be kind without being cruel.

When Georg publishes his findings, the foundations of the world tremble and logic is shaken, but the fear of Georg's contemporaries does not stop him. It is not his place to care for the old cathedrals and the crowns of kings. If his ideas defy determinism and materialism, then those concepts must disappear. The intellectual stunted of his time rend their garments. For this, Georg is harshly criticized, caricatured, and insulted. The doors of the universities are closed to him, many of his colleagues ridicule his work, and not a few editors of mathematics journals refuse to publish him. They were all terrorized by the face of God, of the gods of the unimaginable. William Blake had understood, but he had died almost sixty years before, vilified by the stupidity of his colleagues.

His closest friends turned their backs on him. Hermann Schwarz, with whom he had formed a twenty-year friendship forged as university classmates, decides to stop corresponding with him. "Not one more letter for that heretic," he confesses in a personal letter. Leopold Kronecker, his professor in the University of Berlin, rejects his articles and declares him an enemy. He publicly sustains that Georg's work can be considered low quality philosophy or theology, but it is certainly not mathematics.

The Voice had warned him: sometimes memory is a shallow grave, sometimes a deep well of hate. Georg knows the problem is not in the emphatic logic of the numbers, but in the needy experience of those condemned to die.

Only his friend Dedekind remains by his side.

Who knows what true loneliness is—
not the conventional word but the naked terror?
To the lonely themselves it wears a mask.
The most miserable outcast hugs
some memory or some illusion.
Joseph Conrad

The day had cooled off by the standards of this city built over the frying pans of hell. After having been in the garden for a while, we made a little trip around the hospital and arrived at his room. It was simple and organized. The bed was next to a window, a poster of *The Wall* hung on the adjacent wall and a desk with papers. On the night table was a wooden chess set and a Bible illuminated by a lance of light that escaped from under the curtain.

At times it was impossible for me to believe that he didn´t remember anything of his most recent years, since the main part of his life had been an act. Marcos was a habitual liar and especially presented his life in an overly dramatic way. He liked to flirt with insanity. I suppose it made him feel special, chosen by the same gods that had spoken to Cantor and to Pink, the protagonist of *The Wall*. I asked him if he knew where he was and he responded, "Yes, in a rest clinic." Then I believed that the charade had ended and that he was taking off the mask. I looked at him satisfied, but his face was a blank.

"I came here a few days ago to rest. Working on my thesis wears me down a lot. You know the same thing happened to Cantor and Gödel, sometimes they were sent to psychiatric hospitals."

"Chesterton used to say that poets don't go crazy, but mathematicians and chess players do, that insanity is a risk of logic and not of imagination," I said.

"It´s because working on the kinds of problems that we work on demands too much. You know, the rigor of logic."

"Logic isn´t rigorous, it´s reductionist. Nothing that is really important can be reduced to a right answer," I argued.

"Anyway," continued Marcos, ignoring my comment. "Since I came in voluntarily, I can leave whenever I want, and so if I need something from the university for my work, I can go in just a sec. Have you been to Montería recently?"

"We are in Montería," I told him, losing my patience and feeling a little guilty. He looked at me surprised and glanced around. He got up from the bed and raised the curtain to look out the window. I did the same and stood there looking at the Bengal's almond leaves on the back wall of the garden.

"It´s very hot," he told me as if he believed that the Monterían heat was not possible in Medellín. I said nothing more for the moment, just looked at the Bengal with my brow furrowed. I couldn't help but think that part of his condition was faked, but this time his pantomime was protected by tragedy. It was impossible to know where maladapted neurons left off and his role as Quixote picked up.

"I want some of my thesis to be informative, to familiarize the general public with Cantor's ideas. You know who he is, right, Avski?"

"You've told me a thousand times," I responded. Marcos nodded with a half-smile and ignored my answer. He immediately started explaining who Georg Cantor was and how his life had been.

At that moment I remembered one night near the end of 1998, already a little drunk, when he confessed to me that he would hear Cantor's voice. By then I was fed up with his constant foolishness and crazy behavior.

"Don't come to me with that bullshit," I had responded. "Does Cantor speak to you in Spanish or German? I hope it's Spanish because it'd be a shame for Cantor to come all the way over from the other side to communicate with you and you don't understand a fucking word."

He looked at me surprised and ended up laughing. He told me

later that it was a joke, that he said it every now and then to see how people would react.

"How big is infinity?" Marcos asked me.

The question brought me back to the present, to the presence of my insane friend. Without giving me time to respond, he said, "The size of God. God is the infinity of infinities. Do you know Cantor believed that only God could have implanted the ideas about infinity in him? Real infinity does not exist anywhere in the universe."

"Like Mafalda, God had to come down from heaven and anoint Himself with the Buenos Aires pollution to inspire Quino or that cartoon would never have existed either."

I imagined Cantor shut away in a psychiatric hospital, in the cold of the German winter, hearing the voice of God or of the devil, desperate to demonstrate his theory's coherence, tormented because his contemporaries didn't give him the recognition he deserved. I looked at Marcos again and wondered if this nut I had in front of me could have really heard the voice of Cantor. I imagined a voice like thunder in the emptiness of a head without memories. Sometimes memory is a grave, sometimes a voice crying out in the desert where no one hears.

Marcos started to speak again, "I'm going to explain it to you with a story I'm using for my thesis." He got up from his chair and looked among some papers on top of his desk. It was obvious that he was in a situation of privilege in the hospital. He had his own room and the privilege of rummaging around in old papers like the shipwrecked debris of his memory. Without any preamble he started to read:

"One night, a traveler arrived at a hotel and asked for a room. The hotel's receptionist informed him that the hotel was full, to which the traveler replied that he had heard that the hotel had infinite rooms, so it didn't make any sense that it was full. Sir, replied the receptionist, we have received infinite guests who have occupied all of the rooms. The traveler, who was an intelligent man, offered the following solution: ask all the guests to move down one room, that is, the guest in room 1 moves down to room 2,

the one in 2 to 3,

the one in 3 to 4,

and so on to infinity.

I can then occupy room 1, which would be left vacant, and we'd all have a place to stay. The receptionist, marveling at the new guest's intelligence, did what he recommended."

"Do you see, Avski? This says that infinity plus one is infinity."

"Later the receptionist received a call from his boss," Marcos continued to read, "who warned him that a party of infinite people was about to arrive at the hotel and that he should find a way to accommodate them all. The desk clerk tried to tell his boss that the hotel was full, and that he had even lodged an additional person, but the hotel owner hung up the phone without listening. So then the receptionist decided to call the guest in room number 1 to pose the problem to him, and this was the answer that he got: ask all of the hotel's guests to multiply their room number by two and move to that room, that is to say, that I'll go to room 2,

the guest staying in room 2 goes to 4,

the one in 3 to 6,

the one in 4 to 8,

the one in 5 to 10,

and so on. In this way you'll have infinite Odd rooms available (1, 3, 5, 7, 9, . . .) for the infinite guests on the way."

"Avski, do you understand? What an easy way to explain that there are as many Odd numbers as there are Naturals, that the Odds are not half."

I nodded without any interest in his story. In reality I had tried to ask him about his family all day, but his rattling about infinity never ended and didn't allow for discussion of anything else. Marcos continued reading indifferently.

"When the receptionist believed that all his problems were

solved he heard a murmur at the hotel entrance and saw people gathering. One person came up to him and told him there was a problem. There was a group traveling all together that needed lodging. They didn't know exactly how many people there were, but they were traveling in infinite buses, each one absolutely full with a capacity for infinite people. The receptionist stood there expressionless and thought about what the guest in room 2 would do.

The first thing he did was to ask, as before, the guests to multiply their room number by two, so that the Odd-numbered rooms would be vacant. The group's delegate argued that that option would barely solve the problem of one of the buses carrying infinite people, to which the receptionist, very proud of his idea, responded that he had not finished.

The people arriving on bus number 1 would stay in rooms 3, 9, 27, 81, that is to say,

3 to the 1

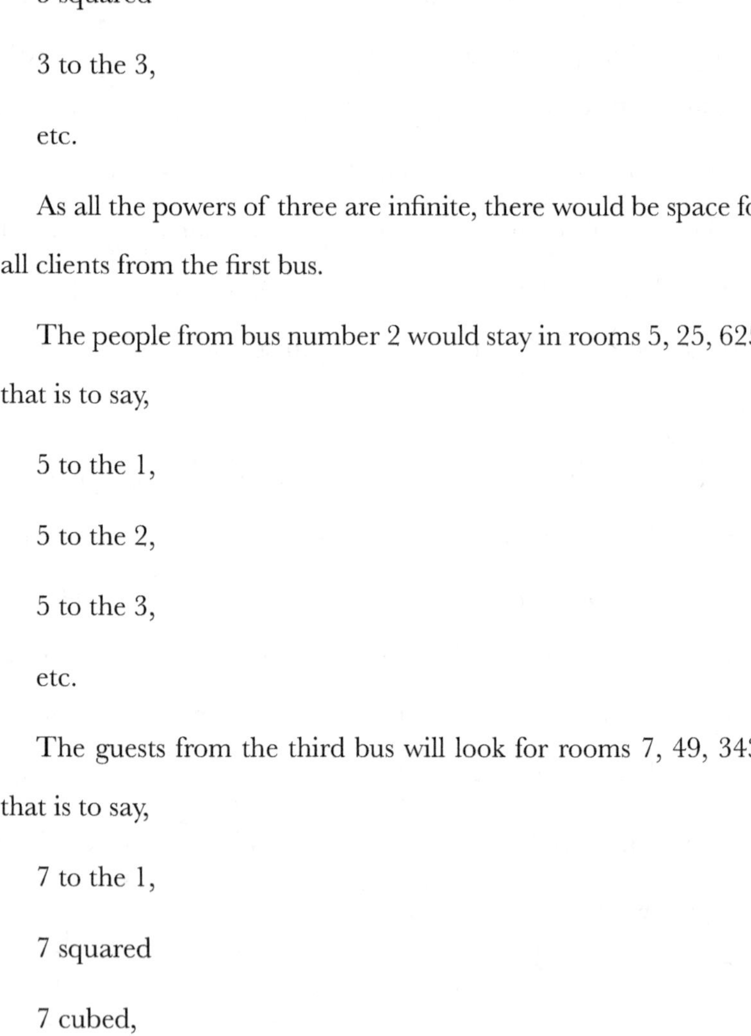

3 squared

3 to the 3,

etc.

As all the powers of three are infinite, there would be space for all clients from the first bus.

The people from bus number 2 would stay in rooms 5, 25, 625, that is to say,

5 to the 1,

5 to the 2,

5 to the 3,

etc.

The guests from the third bus will look for rooms 7, 49, 343, that is to say,

7 to the 1,

7 squared

7 cubed,

etc.

Since there are infinite prime numbers there will be a series of powers for each bus, and since the powers of the prime numbers don't have common factors, no room will be assigned twice.

The receptionist was happy with his solution because not only had he lodged all the customers, but he had also opened infinite vacancies with all Odd numbers that weren't powers of primes. This is to say that the infinity of infinity continues to be infinity of the same size."

Marcos let the pages drop on the chess set and asked me, "Ah? And what do you think? Fascinating, right?"

"I think if Cantor could hear you, he'd be proud," I answered. "Although Hilbert would be angry."

I asked him if he still played chess and he told me that he got bored with it since he couldn't find a rival at his level. Doctor Urbino had explained that in reality his memory didn't allow him to play like before and he always lost. The doctor confessed that for a while, he tried to use the game as an exercise to strengthen Marcos' memory; nevertheless, his mammillary bodies had so deteriorated that the benefits weren't worth the great frustration Marcos experienced.

א

There is no greater pain than
to remember happy times in misery.
Dante Alighieri

Georg tries to prove a relationship between the infinities. This test becomes the center of his life, his principal objective. The Hypothesis of the Continuum, he calls it. The Voice explains that the test was the brick that would make his theory indestructible against his detractors and untouchable to the unbelievers.

The argument is simple. He had already shown that other infinities like the Rationals that seemed to be larger or smaller like the Odds, in reality are the same size as the Natural numbers. They are the smallest size of infinity, which is named ℵ0 using the letter Aleph that for his Jewish ancestors represented the unity of God. He also showed that the Reals, the numbers that skirmish among themselves like snakes in a nest until no spaces are left, are much more numerous than the Naturals. They are a larger sized infinity, more distant, crueler. He named that one $\aleph 1$. Georg found a complete hierarchy of infinities progressively larger, but what he wanted to show was that there was no other size of infinity between $\aleph 0$ and $\aleph 1$, that no god inhabited the space between the Naturals and their cousins, the Real numbers.

He retreats in silence for two years. He only listens to the Voice that changes, disappears, and reappears without order. Sometimes it is clear, other times cryptic and rough. On occasion, it speaks in arcane languages and sometimes it remains silent.

One rainy afternoon during rest, while he was smoking his pipe next to the window, he heard it clearly and deeply. It revealed marvelous details that no man before had seen with the naked eye, which Georg transcribed to paper with tear-filled eyes. Until then he had thought the plane would be of infinite size following straight away, but that afternoon the Voice revealed to him that there were as many points in a piece of a line as in a plane that expands without limit beyond the borders of the universe. Even still, he clearly saw there are as many numbers hiding in the wasteland of a straight line than in all that exists in three-dimensional space. Georg could not help but be surprised. In the scant, tiny cosmos that exists between two points on a piece of paper there is enough space for all the tragedy contained in the whole universe, including all the hidden dimensions and the dark secrets of the human heart hidden on the banks of the river of time.

For his detractors this result is proof of the degradation that Georg has introduced into the center of mathematics, but for Georg it was no more than a description of how God inhabits the narrowness of our hearts. The search for truth has left me alone, he writes to Dedekind. My friends have turned their backs on me without even listening to my arguments. My critics are unjust and, I suspect, malicious. I feel like the whole world is against me. Johann Friedrich Herbart demands that transfinite numbers have the same properties that the finites possess, and when he does not find them, he denounces the contradiction. Herbart may as well demand that God be mortal and human and conclude that He does not exist because He doesn´t comply with his demands. Gauss' followers have come out again against my work. Cauchy's disciples and all the positivist school find that my work errs mathematically and threatens religious doctrine. Pope Leon XIII considers me a blasphemer and Cardinal Franzelin has requested that I stop writing to him. Is my search for God heresy?

The Voice was warm on a cold, dry afternoon when he decided to walk around the Saale River. That day he felt like the rigging that suspended him by a thread was at the breaking point and his entire being would break into a thousand pieces like a clock that falls to the floor. In the depths of the grove, the Voice calmed and reminded him that God was at his side, and He would not give him a task that he was not capable of handling. He reminded him that his eyes had seen forms that still remained hidden to other men before and after him.

Other times the Voice was cryptic and rough, like the night that He spoke to him in dreams and showed him a road in the woods, full of haze and stalking forms. In the hollows of the thickets were dead men clutching rifles and wild dogs eating their fill of rotten meat. The woods ended in others, darker and more threatening, colder, more fetid, and desolate. There, the dead walked, dragging their feet through muddy trenches. The dogs chased them and ripped out chunks of flesh in single bites. From those woods extended others even worse, and from those, more without end. Each forest contained the previous, each odor was composed of those previous, and each predator ate of the putrid flesh of all the preceding animals.

The Voice was sibilant on a bright morning when He spoke to Georg after reading correspondence. He explained that all his detractors had been touched by the same obscure hand. He spoke of long-coming justice to be found in the graves reserved for heretics and traitors, but Georg did not know if the place was reserved for him for having destroyed the pillars of logic, or for his enemies for defying the will of the God of infinity.

Other times he heard remote languages no human had ever heard before. Celestial argot, hellish laments, voices of lost civilizations, dialects of other worlds and other races. On one of those occasions, the Voice spoke to him of William Shakespeare and Francis Bacon for the first time, although without advancing too many details.

At home he does not speak with anyone, and only responds with a blank stare. His only contact with the world is the correspondence with Dedekind in which they discuss his work and where he learns about the slanders against him.

lost the passion for carnal pleasures, as well as the appetite for the intellectual ones. He would drink without thirst, eat without hunger, and stopped smoking and chasing women. Suddenly, books bored him, the cinema seemed a waste of money, and even traveling to other countries seemed pointless. It was music only that continued to bring him joy.

He would deliberately set up the few meetings we did have, where we would argue until he would get irritated, or I would humiliate him for his academic failure. Marcos usually reacted with violence. Other times he would try to make peace and act like the mature person that neither of us was, which would irritate me even more. I would try to make sure that he would never again look for me, and for a while, it worked.

One night we ran into each other accidently. I was pretty wasted. and Marcos didn´t waste any time leveling up with me. In the early morning hours we started talking about his love life. It was half discussion between friends, half malicious conversation. I told him I thought he was gay or bisexual, and as long as he didn't admit it, he would not have a good relationship with anyone. I said it with the intention of making him angry, under the stupid assumption that it would imply an insult. He told me no. He said he liked women, but there was a childhood trauma he couldn't get over. He warned me that it was the first time he spoke honestly on the subject. He assured me that when he was a kid, his grandmother had told him that his father was not his real father; in reality, no one knew who his real father was since his mother went to bed with everybody, which led to her death. He also confessed that when he was ten years old, his grandmother offered soft drinks to workers repairing the street in front of her house. One afternoon she paid one of the workers to rape him and when the worker finished, she dressed him like a girl and took him out in the street so all the workers would make fun of him.

"I don´t believe a single word," I said.

"Avski. . ." he said, with his eyes full of tears.

"We´re too old for this much drama," I said angrily and left.

א

I sensed that my sword was conquered by age,
and I could find nothing on which to fix my gaze
that was not a reminder of death.
Francisco de Quevedo

I never saw him again until the day I saw him in the hospital. A little while after our last meeting, Marcos moved to Bogotá. He had been staying away from all the old friends from Montería, so his social life was just about nonexistent. He only kept in contact with Luis Otero, with who he started hanging out in the capital.

I found out that he started studying history at the National University. He contacted two professors from Montería, Anwar Abdallah and Antonio Ayala, who were in the mathematics department. He wanted to write a dissertation on Georg Cantor and asked them to advise him on the project. Somehow he convinced them that he had finished his mathematics degree at the University of Antioquia, but because his advisor did not understand his thesis, he hadn´t graduated. Marcos made so much noise about his project that it was rumored he would get an honorary doctorate once he finished it. But, of course, it´s more likely that he hadn´t even started writing it and he had started the rumor. That´s how he was. Anyway, the dissertation was never finished because Marcos quit the program before the end of the first year and left to study English in Jamaica for six months.

Jamaica was a dark time in his life and little is known about it. Sometimes memory is a deep grave, sometimes a stamp in a passport.

Once he returned he agreed to rent an apartment with Luis Otero. They chose the neighborhood around Seventh and Seventy-second and a few days later they moved. He wanted to return to studying History of Mathematics at one of the universities on the

Bogotá savanna.

Getting along wasn´t easy. Marcos returned to Colombia too late to get into any universities, so he spent all day in the apartment. Luis explained that he would wake up in the middle of the night to find Marcos in the living room listening to Pink Floyd records with headphones on. The first night he was woken by desperate sobs. Scared, he approached to see what was happening, but Marcos never knew Luis was there. He continued, absorbed in the universe of music, crying as if some tragedy had just occurred. Suddenly the weeping turned into cackling laughter and Marcos started to shout. He called some women awful names and laughed his ass off. One time Luis could recognize the names of Marcos´ grandmother and mother and many other women he didn´t know.

Luis said that his tidiness had disappeared. He would go days without bathing and when he did, he didn´t always change clothes. He never washed the dishes or cleaned the house. In those days, Luis never saw him go out. He would order food on the phone and stayed in his room all day. Pizza boxes and half-eaten containers of Chinese food would pile up in there. He only left the apartment twice. The first time was the day Luis organized a meeting so all his old Montería friends could come visit him. Marcos took off that afternoon before the guests arrived and didn´t come back until the next day.

The second time was when he went to the cash machine to take out money to pay the rent.

Luis might have told me other things that I've forgotten. Maybe he´s forgotten some things, too. The third or fourth weekend after Marcos returned they went out drinking. When they got back to the apartment, Marcos confessed to having had a homosexual relationship in Jamaica, but the next day, and forever after that, he denied it.

They had a fight a little while after that and Marcos moved out to another place.

א

A casual stroll through the lunatic asylum
shows us that faith doesn´t prove anything.
Friedrich Nietzsche

One day he thinks that the Voice has lied to him. Georg proves the Continuum Hypothesis to be false. That is tantamount to setting fire to his own cathedral and destroying his own work. He searches for silence and winds up walking through the woods alongside the river. Those are the days just before the beginning of summer and the trees are intensely green. Georg observes how the light still manages to find its way around the foliage and some lances of light hit the forest floor. He does not know if he should be honest and publish his work or hide it like the Pythagoreans.

Despite the silence of nature the Voice is not silent; it speaks to him in a coarse Hebrew, sometimes vulgar, sometimes infantile, but Georg ignores it. He understands the Voice that speaks to him is that of the Evil One. His mission has taken mathematics to the limit of uncertainty, precisely the mathematics that is the only human port where logic can dock. He has destroyed the only certainty in the teeming sea of perplexities that is the life of man. In front of him, destroyed by his own hand, is the only map that leads to the true God. Looking at the waters of the Halle River, he thinks of a mirror and imagines himself reflected as the Antichrist, the one responsible for the condemnation of an entire race. Henri Poincaré, a brilliant mathematician and one of his main detractors, was right when he pointed out that his ideas were a weed that had to be eradicated from mathematics.

Two days later he finds an error in his argument. His work was intact, his cathedral still standing and the way to God open to the pilgrim´s steps. He goes out to walk through the woods, this time satisfied, smiling like a child. He asks his son to go with him and shows him the path beside the river. That afternoon he tells him about the mission God has assigned to him. He also tells him of his detractors and explains that they are not evil men; some are notable mathematicians like Kronecker and Poincaré, but they acted like scared animals before the vastness of God. Lastly, he asks his son to look at the columns of light that pierce the foliage and to remember that they are much higher than his eyes can see, extending beyond the forest to the atmosphere and all the way to the heart of the sun.

The following day he resumes his work with the same vigor, although his nerves are slow to calm down. Hours and days pass. A few months later he believes that he has proven the Continuum Hypothesis, only to discover later that there is an error in his proof. In the background, like far-off music, he always hears the murmur of his critics. Those lightweight intellectuals don´t cease to run scared. For them it must be like seeing a man hold the universe in the palm of his hand, a trick only imagined possible with Burizaco´s help.

For a while the Voice changed, transformed into many voices, like a legion. Other times, it is not Jehovah who he hears, but his enemies. "And what if all this time it has been the Beast who has been speaking to me?" Georg asks himself. "And what if infinity is the face of Beelzebub and not Yahweh? And if God were the music that I abandoned to pursue the mathematic way?"

The voices against Georg are many. They murmur everywhere. They call him heretic or fool. They scorn him in public, a circus of hatred and envy. They are all hypocrites who would have liked to have touched God with such delicacy, to see God's face in the desperation of the night, but in private they admire the cathedral whose walls never end, or cry, fearful that their names are not written in the Creator´s infinite eyes.

Georg writes to his editor Mittag-Leffler, on December 23, 1883: Dear friend, those that call themselves mathematicians can think of my ideas whatever they like. They can write to Paris or London, or to Kamchatka if it makes them happy, to conspire against me, but I am sure the intelligent minds of future generations will be dedicated to the ideas I am working on with the strength I have left, even when I and my dear friends, the honorable mathematicians, have gone down the road of all mortals. I am far from attributing my discoveries to my personal merit, because I am nothing more than an instrument of a superior power that will continue its work long after my days.

A few months later, in May of 1884, Georg suffers a nervous breakdown and is admitted to Halle Nervenklinik, a rest clinic not far from his Halle house.

א

To me, every hour of the light
and dark is a miracle.
Walt Whitman

Doctor Urbino told me many details of Marcos' life after we had lost contact. Not being able to graduate from his mathematics program caused a lot of conflict. Marcos felt he could not reconcile the idea he had about himself with what his academic failure projected. That took him to Bogotá and Jamaica, where he could not put the pieces together again.

Back in the miserable heat of Montería, Marcos tried to find work at the University of Córdoba. Of course, he had neither the political credentials necessary to traffic in favors, nor the minimal academic titles to get a job. So he decided to lie. He presented himself as a mathematician from the University of Antioquia with a Masters in Epistemology and History of Mathematics from National University of Tres de Febrero in Argentina. When they asked for his diplomas and transcripts, he explained that the University of Antioquia had made a mistake they still hadn´t corrected, and that his Masters diploma would arrive any day from Buenos Aires.

But when they received a negative response from the university, he was already a math teacher for fourth and fifth grade students at the Camino del saber School in the Buena Vista neighborhood. He got in with a fake diploma that he had made for himself at a woodworking shop.

His days as a teacher were possibly the happiest of his adult life. He organized a chess club with his students that met on Tuesday and Thursday afternoons. Soon after he moved the club to the old Flores Street, a block shy of the Palabras bar, and open it to children from any school. In those days, when he ran into some old acquaintance who asked about his math achievements, he would quickly come up with the excuse that he was much more interested in the education of future generations than the vanity of academic life.

Around the middle of February, Marcos and his students made plans to attend the national chess championships in Villavicencio. He had rarely been seen so active. The club ran on a scant budget that Marcos put together with voluntary student donations and private classes. To collect the trip money, he did workshops in schools, attended social events, visited local businesses and large chains, and organized raffles and bazaars. He collected the money in record time and threw himself into preparing his students over Christmas break so they would shine in the competition.

A week before the start of the national chess championship, Marcos disappeared.

Nothing was known of him for nearly a year.

Sometimes memory is a shallow grave, and sometimes that is

all that it is.

He had abandoned his job in Montería to teach math in a newly opened German school in Barranquilla, where he taught basic calculus to students who had decided to study engineering. It was a year of personal satisfaction in which he recovered his confidence. Nevertheless, the work didn´t last long.

Before the end of his first year, a student´s parent wanted to dust off his German with the newly arrived professor from Bavaria. Marcos couldn't respond, and as much as he tried to conceal that he didn´t know a word of the German language, the incident awakened suspicions and soon after he was asked to resign.

In Medellín, Marcos had bought a false diploma in which the University of Göttingen granted him the title of Doctor of Mathematics. It was the same university where Georg Cantor had wanted to be a professor but was never offered a job.

April is the cruelest month, breeding
lilacs out of the dead land, mixing
memory and desire, stirring
dull roots with spring rain.
T.S. Eliot

Marcos returned to Medellín, started to drink, and worked in a mechanic shop. His memory silently deteriorated and it was common for him to not remember what he did while he was drunk. Sometimes he lost control and got violent. He was in jail a couple of times for public scandals. Things drunks do, nothing serious.

Some years passed, life passed and above all, death passes and the terrible history of Colombia. Mathematics remained out of

Marcos′ life during those years. Chess, too. In March of 2009, he checked into the Imperio 70 hotel, close to the Atanasio Girardot Sports Complex. He paid for just one night but never checked out. When the employees found him, they thought he was dead and called the police, sure it had been a murder.

The police discovered that Marcos was alive, and he was transported to the Soma clinic. The doctors concluded that he had tried to kill himself with a cocktail of pills and alcohol but erred in his calculations.

By then the death of Marcos mattered not to the rest of the world. He had neither friends nor family and did nothing significant in his life or in that of any other. His grandmother and aunt preferred to know nothing of him; as for his fellow employees, he was nothing more than a fellow employee. A new folder with legal forms in a moldy box at the police station would have been the most radical change his death would have brought to the world.

His intellectual and sentimental frustrations had rendered

him incapable of relating to anyone. He was left dried up on the inside. Marcos was nothing more than a shell. He felt no passion whatsoever, shared nothing with anyone, and enjoyed no secret pleasure. He would get up in the morning, go to the workshop where he avoided talking about himself, ate lunch with neither pleasure nor disgust, and finished his workday with the same disinterest. After, he would sit in a bar or a shop to drink, indifferent to the enjoyment of the liquor, invisible to the arcane spirits freed by his libations.

In reality, Marcos had died a while ago. This fool without memory in the psychiatric hospital, betrayed by the discontinuity of his memories, was much more alive than the one who attempted suicide. Forgetting was the only possible contract with life.

I remember at some point, years after our last meeting, I got a call from him. Maybe it was some months before the suicide attempt, maybe only a few days before, maybe it was that same night, I don't know. Sometimes memory is a shallow grave, sometimes an imprecise instrument.

At the time, I was glad to hear his voice and to know how he was. By then he had lost contact with all our Montería friends and no one had known anything of him for years. He told me that he was writing a biography on Cantor that included readings of his works that no other biographer had ever revealed. I asked him if he had already started writing and he said, no, but he had it in his head, which was eighty percent of the work. To keep the dialogue going I told him that it was hard work for me to get those books out of my head and onto paper. "We're not all the same, Avski," he responded. "It'll take me no more than two months to write it."

He talked about publication offers, independent math projects, and educational programs for television. In those days he must have been working in the automotive shop, but he told me that he was writing articles without signing them for a cultural magazine. Pretty soon I was fed up listening to the same bullshit as always and interrupted the conversation. "Marcos, I don't believe you for shit," was the last thing I said to him. Since then, I heard no news of him until I came to the hospital to research the poet Raúl

Gómez Jattin, and I found him here by accident.

By the time Marcos carried out his suicide attempt, the mammillary bodies of his brain—the parts in charge of short-term memory and the first active elements to store our new memories, had already been systematically destroyed by several years of strongly abusing alcohol. Finally, the suicide attempt stripped the problem bare. It is known as Korsakoff Syndrome.

In Marcos´ case, the doctor explained, his syndrome was accompanied by a very odd type of amnesia for which they did not have a satisfactory explanation. The incapacity to register new events explained why Marcos didn't remember anything that had happened to him since his attempted suicide. His amnesia extended much further into the past, to about the middle of 1998, when Marcos was still a mathematics student and maintained a certain emotional equilibrium.

The doctor told me that with his aunt's help they could validate the precision of Marcos´ memories from years past at the border of his memories. His memory turned out to be extraordinarily exact. He could give tiny details of events with which he had no sentimental attachment and that had happened fifteen or twenty years prior.

I could also corroborate. He remembered my phone numbers in Medellín and Montería, my cell phone number, my class schedule, and the exact price of a Pavese book we bought together in the Bastilla Passage, a gallery of used books in downtown Medellín. He remembered my birthdate and those of my brother and sister. He repeated my father's license plate number and the exact roster of the Colombian national team that beat Argentina 5 to 0 in the Monumental, with the accurate minutes and seconds when the goals were scored.

According to the doctor, Marcos was not conscious of his lack of memory, although he sometimes expressed anxiety and powerlessness when faced with the contradictions produced as a consequence of his state. Maybe he had come to develop a sense of familiarity with the hospital grounds and the people around him. For Marcos, the hospital personnel, the nurse he saw daily, for instance, was like stranger he ran into often. Somebody he didn't know who turned out to be familiar.

A year ago he suffered an episode of dementia. He woke up one night shouting that he heard voices. In the interview with the doctor the following morning, he told him that there had been two voices speaking to him: that of Georg Cantor and that of God. Both revealed mathematical results to him. The interview continued for about two hours, during which the doctor was surprised that Marcos could sustain a coherent and continuous discourse for so much time.

"Naturally, the subject of the voices alarmed me, but above all, I was interested in how his memory seemed to function well," remembered the doctor. "He spoke as if he were conscious of what he had said an hour before. Of course, it is something that I cannot prove, but it was very obvious. About two hours into the interview, he excused himself to go to the bathroom and when he returned to the room, he already couldn't remember anything. Since then, he hasn´t experienced an episode like that one."

Sometimes memory is a shallow grave, sometimes it's an even shallower dirty puddle.

I asked the doctor if there was any possibility for Marcos to recover his memory. "None, I believe," he admitted. "But his quality of life can improve if we can create an adequate emotional environment."

I asked if anyone had visited him and he said only his aunt. She came several times and her visits had a very positive effect, but after an argument she never returned. According to Marcos, his aunt was not being honest with the handling of the money that remained from his mother's life insurance. In reality, he only had a right to the money until he was twenty-six, but Marcos didn't know how many years were rotting in the trash can of his memory.

The Library is a sphere whose exact center
is any one of its hexagons and whose
circumference is inaccessible.
Jorge Luis Borges

There is no smallest among the small, and no
largest among the large, but always
something still smaller and something still larger.
Anaxagoras

Recovery is rapid. Around the end of May in that same year Georg is back home but is incapable of continuing his mathematic work. He dedicates himself to philosophy and theology, and fights Thomism and its ridiculous positions regarding infinity. He agrees with the rector of the University of Halle to leave his mathematics chair and move to philosophy.

The change suits me, he confessed to Dedekind in a letter during that time. I feel motivated and emotionally stable. The response of my students is positive and the classroom discussions are much more stimulating for me than the opinions of my mathematician friends. Many of my students actively participate and one is interested, although it may be tangentially, in my transfinite numbers.

Georg feels a new beginning.

In those days the Voice reveals to him that it was the philosopher Francis Bacon who wrote many of the works attributed to William Shakespeare. Georg sets out to reveal the literary supplanting. He returns to studying like in the days of the Continuum Hypothesis. He studies in detail the works of the philosopher and the playwright, confronting sources, finding consistent logical patterns, traces of common arguments, and stubborn linguistic matrices. As a result of this investigation he starts writing two articles that he will present at a symposium years later.

With time he also resumes his scientific labor. He sends new results to his editor Mittag-Leffler, but he responds that he cannot publish them since the work is more philosophical than mathematic. Georg understands that Mittag-Leffler has also turned his back on him and the pages of his journal are forever closed. Also, in those days, the mathematician Felix Klein invites him to collaborate on the *Mathematische Annalen* journal, for which Georg produces some articles about problems less demanding for his mental health. After a few months he recovers confidence in his intellectual faculties and the stability of mood necessary to face serious mathematics problems. He still wants to prove the Continuum Hypothesis, but the proof is as elusive as before. Each new failure pushes him away from mathematics. The Voice goes silent for some months and it unbalances him emotionally. He never knows his efforts are as useless as tilling the sea, because years after his death another mathematician touched with genius and insanity would demonstrate that the Continuum Hypothesis cannot be proven.

Despite this, Georg does not return to the sanatorium.

Not yet.

On December 16, 1899, while Georg is giving a talk on Bacon and the authorship of Shakespeare's works, his youngest son dies. At that moment the Voice abandons him for good, as if the Voice and the heartbeats of his son were one. Sometimes memory is a shallow grave, sometimes it is the pain of a father.

Back in his home in Halle, Georg sits down to write two letters under the light of the teardrop lamp. The first is to Dedekind or to Klein, we will never know for sure. The letter is lost to history. We will never know its content either, although it would be easy to guess that it encompasses the pain that he feels over the death of his son.

The second goes to the German Minister of Education. In it, he requests that he be relieved of his responsibilities as a professor and that instead they offer him a position in a modest library, or where they consider pertinent. Georg believes that it is very important that he does not have to face a group of students, answer questions, or do public presentations. He writes of Bacon, Shakespeare, and the King of England. He asserts they share a terrible secret that could endanger the security of the entire British Empire. Lastly, he promises that if his request is not accepted, he will be obliged to join the Russian diplomatic corps, against German interests.

In the succeeding days he received a letter from Felix Klein, his friend and new editor. It would be an answer to one of the two letters he wrote as a consequence of his son's death, or maybe not. Klein shows himself to be worried about Georg's mental health and suggests to Georg to take a rest, a vacation with his wife and children, and abandon his philosophical and mathematical research for a while.

Georg ignores his advice.

As one would expect, the German Minister of Education never responds, so Georg continues as a professor at the University of Halle and never joins the Russian diplomatic service. He soon returns to the sanatorium where, without the Voice, he feels alone. God, or the devil, punishes him with silence. Then come years of emptiness, of instability, of trips back and forth to psychiatric clinics. He often dreams of his dead son and returns with him to the path next to the Halle River. Tired of coming and going Georg decides that he prefers not to return home, although he was medically cleared to do so. A new century is Europe's hope, but not for Georg, who from the window of the tower next to the Halle Nervenklinik sanatorium, sees war approaching as if it were the darkness of night.

During this period, he is invited to give talks on mathematics in many parts of Europe. Sometimes he accepts, other times he feels weak and fears a relapse. When he agrees, he surprises the attendees with arguments about the authorship of Shakespeare's works that have nothing to do with the marvels of infinity they all hope to hear. His talks are always eccentric, disorganized, and circular: Bacon, God, Shakespeare, infinity. He tells them about the coming war, of the roar he hears from the window of his tower. The bewilderment is so great that most of the time Georg does not realize a generation of young mathematicians exists who recognize his genius and want to continue his legacy.

One day he disappears in London looking for the definitive proof that shows the philosopher and playwright, like God and infinity, are one. Like the proof of the Continuum Hypothesis before, it also escapes him. He reappears three days later near the English parliament, dressed in clothing that is not his and covered in chicken shit.

Years pass, get entangled, and life passes in the sanatorium and the conferences, along with the terrible history of the devastation of Europe. Georg dies on January 6, 1918, malnourished by the lack of supplies due to the war, forgotten in the tower next to the Halle Nervenklinik.

Suicides are timid murders.

Cesare Pavese

To listen to Marcos was even more tiresome than before. He didn't stop talking about his thesis, about God, about the infinities, about Cantor. He spoke in circles and said the same things repeatedly with almost the same words. I interrupted him to ask about Petite Margot, and he told me he didn't know who I was talking about. It was strange that he didn't remember since she was clearly from the period he could describe in surprising detail. When I reminded him of the relationship with her, he interrupted me, bewildered, "Avksi, I believe you are confused."

I remember the doctor had told me that his amnesia had to

do with his Korsakoff Syndrome, but that it was also a significant component of hysteria. Many of his memories had disappeared, not because they had been affected by physical damage to his brain, but due to psychological defense mechanisms.

I asked him if he remembered Anwar Abdallah and Antonio Ayala, the professors from the National University with whom he wanted to work when he studied history.

"I haven't seen them in a long time," he responded.

I asked him if he remembered his parents, and for the first time, he gave me a direct response.

"Not much," he said.

He told me they were named Helena Pupo and Darío Lyons and were killed when he was a child. When I asked him why they had been killed, he responded that they were members of the Patriotic Union. He went silent for a few seconds and added, "Have I told you that my grandfather was French?"

"Why didn't you live with them before they were killed?"

"Who told you they were killed?"

"You told me they were killed for being part of the Patriotic Union."

"That's not true."

"So why did they kill them?"

"Because my mother was a prostitute and my father was gay."

"Why did you tell me they were part of the Patriotic Union?"

He didn't answer. I don't remember anything else and I don't care. I asked thousands of questions that he didn't answer or didn't remember. When I was leaving the hospital the doctor asked me if I would be returning to visit Marcos. He explained how important it was to his quality of life to have periodic visits.

"Of course," I lied. Maybe Marcos should have used the razor blade he showed me once, I thought, as I walked out the door. For Marcos, the worst continued: life without meaning. Sometimes memory is a shallow grave, sometimes a door that closes, never to be opened again.

AUTHOR'S BIOGRAPHY

Joseph Avski

Born in Medellín, Colombia. Joseph graduated with a degree in Physics from the Universidad de Antioquia (Colombia), an MFA in Creative Writing from University of Texas at El Paso, and a Ph.D in Hispanic Studies from Texas A&M. He has published poetry and short stories in Colombia, Argentina, Chile, Uruguay, Spain, Mexico, and the USA. He has won short story contests in Colombia, Uruguay, and the USA. In 2009, he won the IX annual National Novel Award from the Medellín Chamber of Commerce with his opera prima *El corazón del escorpión* (Published in English as *Heart of Scorpio*). In 2010, he was the finalist in the XII Novel Biennial "José Eustasio Rivera" with his novel *El libro de los infiernos (The Book of Infernos)*. His memoir about his time in El Paso, *A un paso de Juárez/ A Step from Juárez*, was also published by Mouthfeel Press in a bilingual edition. *Infinity End Soon*, was published in 2015 in Colombia and is part of the literature curriculum in schools all over the country. Joseph is currently an associate professor at Northwest Missouri State University.

TRANSLATOR'S BIOGRAPHY

Mark McGraw

Born in Ft. Worth, Texas, Mark McGraw attended Texas A&M University where he earned a Ph.D. in Hispanic Studies in 2013. He is a writer, translator, and language professor. He is the author of *Behind Friendly Lines: Memoirs of a US Marine in Chile* (Lucid 2019). He is the translator of Joseph Avski´s novel *El corazón del escorpión* (*Heart of Scorpio*, Tiny Toe 2012) and memoir *A un paso de Juárez* (*One Step from Juárez*, Mouthfeel 2015). He lives in Waco, Texas.

www.ingramcontent.com/pod-product-compliance
Lightning Source LLC
Chambersburg PA
CBHW070512200726
48293CB00007B/2505

9781957840017